smithton church

Presents this book to

Millie Gray

At Sunday Club Prize Giving

on 24th June 2018

Signed: *[signature]*

(Alasdair Macleod: Minister)

- - - - - - - - -

- - - - - - - - -

For Steve   L.R.
To my sister Paola   A.M.

Text by Lois Rock
Illustrations copyright © 2016 Alida Massari
This edition copyright © 2016 Lion Hudson

The right of Alida Massari to be identified as the illustrator of this work has been asserted by her in accordance with the Copyright, Designs and Patents Act 1988.

Published by Lion Children's Books
an imprint of
Lion Hudson plc
Wilkinson House, Jordan Hill Road,
Oxford OX2 8DR, England
www.lionhudson.com/lionchildrens

ISBN 978 0 7459 6495 9

First edition 2016

Acknowledgments
The unattributed prayers are by Lois Rock, copyright © Lion Hudson.

Bible extracts are taken or adapted from the Good News Bible © 1994 published by the Bible Societies/HarperCollins Publishers Ltd UK, Good News Bible © American Bible Society 1966, 1971, 1976, 1992. Used with permission.

The Lord's Prayer (p. 70) as it appears in *Common Worship: Services and Prayers for the Church of England* (Church House Publishing, 2000) is copyright © The English Language Liturgical Consultation and is reproduced by permission of the publisher.

A catalogue record for this book is available from the British Library

Printed and bound in China, November 2015, LH06

The Bible and Me

Retold by Lois Rock * Illustrated by Alida Massari

LION
CHILDREN'S

Contents

THE OLD TESTAMENT

The New Testament

In the beginning

The world and all that is in it belong to the Lord.

PSALM 24:1

IN THE BEGINNING was nothing: more shapeless and shifting than a dark and wild ocean. Nothing, nothing, nothing…

… and God. "Let there be light," God cried aloud. The light came sparkling into being. God separated the light from the dark. He named the light "Day" and the dark "Night". That was the very first day.

On the second day God made the sky – a sheltering dome in a vast universe – and on the third, God commanded the land to rise up from the sea.

In the darkness of the soil, the plants uncurled their roots and pushed out shoots. They unfurled their leaves and unfolded their flowers.

God made the sun that lights the day and the moon and stars that shine in the night. Once again evening passed and morning came: the fourth day of creation.

On the fifth day, God spoke again: "Let creatures of every kind swim in the seas, and birds fly through the clear air."

As the sixth day dawned, God called into being every kind of animal, from the smallest to the largest, from the gentlest to the wildest.

"And now," said God, "I shall make people in my own image, who will know that they are my children."

"This world is for you," God told them. "I am putting you in charge of the world I have made, and it will give you everything you need."

The sixth day turned to twilight. God looked at everything he had made and was pleased.

On the seventh day, God stopped working. "Now and evermore the seventh day is special," said God. "It must be a day of rest: time to enjoy the wonderful world I have made."

PRAISE THE LORD from heaven,
all beings of the height!
Praise him, holy angels
and golden sun so bright.

Praise him, silver moonlight,
praise him, every star!
Let your praises shine
throughout the universe so far.

Praise the Lord from earth below,
all beings of the deep!
Lightning, flash! You thunder, roar!
You ocean creatures, leap.

Praise him, hill and mountain!
Praise him, seed and tree.
Praise him, all you creatures
that run the wide world free.

Let the mighty praise him.
Let the children sing.
Men and women, young and old:
Praise your God and king.

FROM PSALM 148

The great flood

As long as the world exists, there will be a time for planting and a time for harvest.

GENESIS 8:22

WHEN GOD FIRST made humankind, the world was good. All too soon, the people chose to go their own way and do wicked things.

As the generations went by, they became more and more violent. "I am sorry I made the world," said God. "I shall send a flood to wipe it out."

There was just one good man. His name was Noah.

God spoke to him. "I want you to build an ark," said God. "It must be big enough for you and your family.

"You must take on board a breeding pair of every kind of living creature, and supplies to last many months."

Noah did everything that God asked him to do.

When everything was ready, God closed the door of the ark. The rain began to fall, and the rivers rose. For forty days and nights the rain came sheeting down from the heavens, and the seas rose and covered all the earth.

In all the world there was nothing but Noah and his ark. Days and weeks and months went by.

God had not forgotten Noah. One day, a wind began to blow. The floodwater began to ebb away. On the seventeenth day of the seventh month, the ark creaked to a stop on the rocks atop Mount Ararat.

One by one, other mountaintops appeared around Noah as the waters sank back to the sea. After forty days, Noah sent out a raven. It simply flew away.

Noah sent out a dove, but it could not find a place to perch and it flew back. Seven days later, Noah sent it out again. The dove returned with a fresh olive leaf in its beak.

"Such good news!" Noah told his family. "A bright new world is emerging from the ooze and slime. Seven days from now, I shall send the bird out again."

The third time the dove flew, it did not come back. It was not many days until the land around the ark was dry.

"It's time to leave the ark," said God. "Set the creatures free, so that they may have young and fill the world again.

"You and your family must make a new home, and farm the land as you used to.

"Never again will I destroy all living beings, as I have done this time. As long as the world exists, there will be a time for planting and time for harvest. There will always be cold and heat, summer and winter, day and night.

"Now and always, the rainbow will be the sign of my solemn promise to all living beings."

O GOD,
You show your care for the land
by sending rain;
you make it rich and fertile.
You fill the streams with water;
you provide the earth with crops.
This is how you do it:
you send abundant rain on the ploughed fields
and soak them with water;
you soften the soil with showers
and cause the young plants to grow.
What a rich harvest your goodness provides!
Wherever you go there is plenty.
The pastures are filled with flocks;
the hillsides are full of joy.
The fields are covered with sheep;
the valleys are full of wheat.
Everything shouts and sings for joy.

PSALM 65:9–13

Abraham's faith

To have faith is to be sure of the things we hope for, to be certain of the things we cannot see.

HEBREWS 11:1

LONG AGO LIVED a man named Abram. He had been born in the city of Ur, in Babylonia. When he was a man, God spoke to him:

"I want you to go to the land of Canaan: you, and all your household. There you will make your home. You will have many descendants, and they will become a great nation.

"Through them, I will bless all the peoples of the world."

Abram had faith in God, and he set out.

There was no welcome in the land of Canaan. The peoples that dwelled there eyed the newcomers mistrustfully. Abram and his household lived as nomads on the wild, uncultivated land, pitching their camp wherever there was pasture for the animals to graze. Each time they did so, they had to dig deep wells to find water, and there was hardly enough for their needs. Even so, this was not the greatest disappointment Abram faced. God had promised he would be the father of a nation… but the years went by and still he and his wife Sarai remained childless.

Abram heard God speaking to him: "Look at the stars in the night sky. One day, your descendants will be as many as the stars – too many to count."

Still the years went by.

Again God spoke: "I am making you a solemn promise, a covenant. You will be known as Abraham, 'father of nations'. The whole land of Canaan will belong to you and your descendants for ever, and I will be their God.

"Your wife Sarai will be known as Sarah: princess. She will have a son, and she will be the mother of my people."

And still time passed: nights that were dark for Abraham and Sarah even though a myriad of stars twinkled above them.

Then, at last, Sarah became pregnant. When her son was born, she laughed for joy.

Abraham named him Isaac, and the name means "laughter".

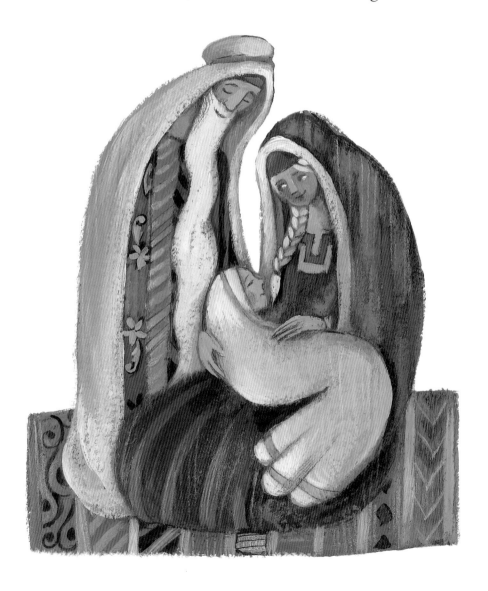

G IVE THANKS TO the Lord; proclaim his
greatness.

The Lord is our God;
his commands are for all the world.
He will keep his covenant for ever,
his promises for a thousand generations.
He will keep the agreement he made
  with Abraham
and his promise to Isaac.

Give thanks to the Lord, because he is good;
his love is eternal.

BASED ON 1 CHRONICLES 16:8, 14–16, 34

Joseph and his dreams

The Lord is God; he has been good to us.

PSALM 118:27

ABRAHAM'S SON ISAAC had two sons, Jacob and Esau. It was Jacob who claimed the blessing from his father: that he and his descendants would be blessed by God.

Jacob in turn planned to pass the blessing on to Joseph, the firstborn of his much-loved wife Rachel. As a sign of his intention, Jacob gave Joseph a splendid cloak.

Jacob had eleven other sons. Benjamin was Rachel's second born. The other ten were sons of other wives. These elder brothers were jealous of Joseph and furious at his arrogance.

24

"I had a dream," said Joseph one day. "I dreamed that we were harvesting in a field. My sheaf of wheat stood up, and your sheaves gathered around and bowed down to it."

The elder brothers sniffed in contempt.

"I had another dream," announced Joseph. "The sun, moon, and eleven stars bowed down to me."

Even Jacob grew angry then. "No," he declared. "Neither I nor your mother nor your brothers will bow down to you."

One day, when Joseph came to visit his elder brothers as they tended the flocks, they turned on him and sold him as a slave to passing traders.

In faraway Egypt Joseph was a nobody, at the mercy of his master. When his master's wife told lies about him, he was thrown into prison.

There Joseph learned to listen to God. This gave him the wisdom to explain dreams. When the ruler of Egypt, the pharaoh, had puzzling dreams, someone sent for Joseph.

Pharaoh told Joseph his dream. "I saw seven fat cows clamber out of the River Nile. Then came seven thin cows that ate the fat ones.

"After that I saw seven plump ears of grain. Seven thin ears swallowed them up."

"The two dreams mean the same thing," Joseph told him. "Seven years of good harvest will be followed by seven years of famine.

"You need to choose someone to store the abundance of the good years to last through the lean years."

At once the Pharaoh put Joseph in charge of the harvests.

When famine struck, his ten elder brothers came to Egypt to buy grain. They bowed low to the stern Egyptian official, not knowing he was their brother.

Joseph knew that the brothers who had so mistreated him were at his mercy.

But the years had changed him. When he found out that his father and his younger brother were still alive, he desperately wanted the family reunited.

"It is time to forgive the past," he said. "God wanted me here in Egypt so I could help you all now. Come and live here, in peace and safety."

So the great-grandchildren of Abraham left Canaan to live in Egypt.

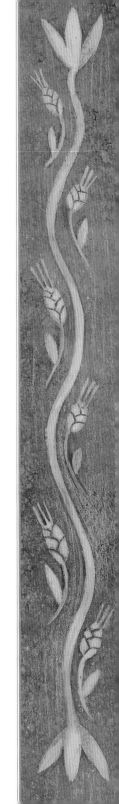

I LOOK TO THE mountains;
where will my help come from?
My help will come from the Lord,
who made heaven and earth.

He will not let you fall;
your protector is always awake.

The protector of Israel
never dozes or sleeps.
The Lord will guard you;
he is by your side to protect you.
The sun will not hurt you during the day,
nor the moon during the night.

The Lord will protect you from all danger;
he will keep you safe.
He will protect you as you come and go
now and for ever.

PSALM 121

Moses and the commandments

God's word is a lamp to guide me and a light for my path.

PSALM 119:105

Moses came hurrying down Mount Sinai. He carried two tablets of stone. On them were engraved the great commandments that God had given to guide his people: the descendants of Abraham and Isaac, the people of Israel.

Moses had every reason to trust in God. It was God who had guided his people to Egypt for safety in the time of Joseph. It was God who had seen when a new pharaoh had made his people slaves. It was God who had kept Moses himself safe from that pharaoh and opened his eyes to the suffering of his people.

It was God who had given Moses the courage and wisdom to lead his people to freedom, and God who had opened a way through the sea as they fled Egypt — a miraculous escape the people would celebrate for always at the festival of Passover.

The commandments that God had given to Moses told the people what they must do to live as God's people. If they obeyed, God would bless them and enable them to make their new home in the land of Canaan. This was the promise, the covenant.

As Moses came near the camp, he heard sounds that troubled him: music, dancing, the yells and whoops of wild celebration.

He hurried closer. What he saw put him in a rage.

The people had made a huge calf of gold and they were holding a festival of worship – as if the lump of metal were a god.

Moses lifted up the tablets of stone and smashed them on the ground. He ordered the festivities to stop at once. How had the people lost faith in their God, he wanted to know? They must be punished severely.

The people soon repented of their wrongdoing.

33

God is always ready to forgive. He called Moses to the top of Mount Sinai and there prepared a second set of tablets. Moses told the people to make a golden box in which to keep the tablets: the ark of the covenant, which would be the greatest treasure of the nation, and the symbol of its faith in God.

O Lord,
I have learned your laws.
May I worship you.
May I worship you alone.
May all I say and do show respect for your holy name.
May I honour the weekly day of rest.
May I show respect for my parents.
May I reject violence so that I never take a life.
May I learn to be loyal in friendship and so learn to be faithful
   in marriage.
May I not steal what belongs to others.
May I not tell lies to destroy another person's reputation.
May I not be envious of what others have, but may I learn to
   be content with the good things you give me.

BASED ON THE TEN COMMANDMENTS, EXODUS 20

God's people

Trust in the Lord and do good;
live in the land and be safe.

PSALM 37:3

WHEN MOSES GREW old, God chose a bold young warrior named Joshua to lead the people into Canaan.

"Be determined and confident," God told him. "Make sure that you obey my laws and commandments. Then you will succeed in everything you do."

The ark of the covenant was carried at the front of the procession that crossed the River Jordan into Canaan. By a miracle, the rush of water slowed to a trickle, and the people walked across.

The ark of the covenant was part of the procession that marched around the walled city of Jericho. By a miracle, the walls fell down. Joshua and his fighting men captured the city.

He went on to capture the entire land. When he grew old, he called the people together. "I and my household will always obey God's laws," he told them. "Will you?"

"We too will obey God," came the reply.

But as the years went by, the people forgot their promise. Time and again they disobeyed God's laws. Time and again enemy nations came and defeated them. Then they pleaded with God for help, and God sent champions to lead them to freedom once more.

Among the enemies of the nation were the Philistines: fierce warriors with bright armour and sharp iron weapons. One day, a giant of a man came swaggering from the Philistine camp. Goliath roared a challenge to the Israelite army.

"If any of you cowards can beat me, you win the war!" he cried.

It so happened that a young shepherd boy named David had come from his home in Bethlehem to visit his soldier brothers that day. He took his sling and five stones from a stream and went to face Goliath.

"I come to you in the name of the mighty God of Israel," he cried. Then he whirled his sling and threw a stone.

The giant fell down. David had won!

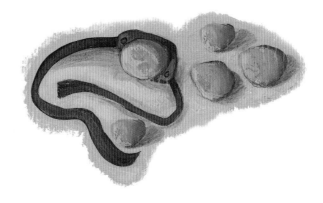

He went on to defeat all of his people's enemies and become king. He chose a hilltop fort to be the capital city of his nation. "Here we will worship God as we should," he declared.

The long-forgotten ark of the covenant was brought in procession into Jerusalem.

David danced for joy, remembering how God had helped him since he was a shepherd boy.

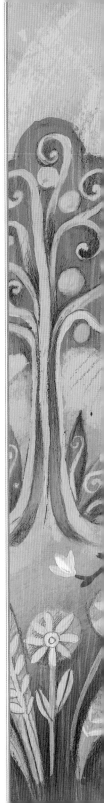

THE LORD IS my shepherd;
I have everything I need.
He lets me rest in fields of green grass
and leads me to quiet pools of fresh water.
He gives me new strength.
He guides me in the right paths,
as he has promised.
Even if I go through the deepest darkness,
I will not be afraid, Lord,
for you are with me.
Your shepherd's rod and staff protect me.

PSALM 23:1–4, A PSALM OF DAVID

Jerusalem

Lord God of Israel… you keep your covenant with your people and show them your love when they live in wholehearted obedience to you.

PRAYER OF KING SOLOMON, 1 KINGS 8:23

KING DAVID BROUGHT the ark of the covenant to Jerusalem, but that was only part of his plan.

He also wanted to build a temple, finely crafted and glittering with gold. It would be a place where the ark would be kept safe in an inner room. Priests would take care of the lamplit interior, and people would come and worship in the courtyard outside.

"It is not you who will build my temple," God told him, "but one of your sons." After David died, his son Solomon became king.

The dedication of the Temple was a moment of national celebration.

The time of devotion to God was short-lived. David had brought the kingdom peace, and Solomon's trading ventures made him wealthy. He grew idle and arrogant, and forgot to obey God's laws.

After he died, some of the people rebelled against his son's rule, and the kingdom was left divided. The kings and people of the northern kingdom soon turned away from God, and it was not many generations before they were defeated by powerful enemies from Assyria and scattered to other lands.

In the southern kingdom of Judah, ruled from Jerusalem, the kings and people remained more faithful in worship, and they survived the Assyrian invasions. As the years went by godlessness increased. The time came when the armies of King Nebuchadnezzar closed in on Jerusalem. They burned the city and its Temple. Many people were taken away to live as exiles in Babylon. The ark of the covenant disappeared in the battle and was never seen again.

Those who wrote the nation's history recorded a warning that God had given Solomon.

"If you or your descendants stop following me… this Temple will become a pile of ruins, and everyone who passes by will be shocked and amazed. 'Why did the Lord do this to this land and this Temple?' they will ask. People will answer, 'It is because they abandoned the Lord their God, who brought their ancestors out of Egypt. They gave their allegiance to other gods and worshipped them. That is why the Lord has brought this disaster on them.'"

O JERUSALEM, BELOVED JERUSALEM,
what can I say?
How can I comfort you? No one has ever suffered like this.
Your disaster is boundless as the ocean; there is no possible hope.

Yet hope returns when I remember this one thing:
The Lord's unfailing love and mercy still continue,
Fresh as the morning, as sure as the sunrise.
The Lord is all I have, and so I put my hope in him.

LAMENTATIONS 2:13 AND 3:21–24

The fiery furnace

I know God is always near me, and nothing can shake me.

FROM PSALM 16:8

K ING NEBUCHADNEZZAR RULED a mighty empire from the city of Babylon. One day, he had a huge gold statue made and set it up in a vast public space outside the city. Then he ordered officials from every province in the empire to attend a grand ceremony.

When everyone had assembled, a herald gave the instructions.

"People of all nations, races, and languages: when you hear the sound of the oboes, lyres, and harps, you are to bow down and worship this statue that King Nebuchadnezzar has set up. Anyone who does not obey this command will be thrown into a blazing, fiery furnace."

Now among those present were three young exiles from the kingdom of Judah. The names of these Jews were Shadrach, Meshach, and Abednego. They were highly respected for their work in King Nebuchadnezzar's government. However, when the musicians began to play, they did not bow down.

"Seize them!" cried some Babylonians. "Take them to the king. If they will not obey his orders, they will face his punishment."

King Nebuchadnezzar glowered at Shadrach, Meshach, and Abednego.

"Is it true that you refuse to bow down to my statue and worship at its feet?" he demanded to know. "If you will not bow down, you will be thrown into a blazing, fiery furnace. Do you think any god can save you from that?"

Shadrach, Meshach, and Abednego stood tall to answer.

"Your Majesty, the charge against us is true. If our God wants to save us from the blazing, fiery furnace, he will.

"But even if he doesn't, you can be sure we will not worship your god. We will not bow down to your golden statue."

King Nebuchadnezzar flew into a rage.

"Tie them up!" he screamed to his soldiers. "Make the furnace seven times hotter than usual. Throw them into the blazing fire."

Shadrach, Meshach, and Abednego tumbled into the flames.

King Nebuchadnezzar watched to see them die. Then he leaped to his feet.

"Were those men not tied up securely? Is the fire not hot enough?

"Look – Shadrach, Meshach, and Abednego are walking among the flames. And there is someone else in there... someone who shines like an angel."

King Nebuchadnezzar was silent for a long moment. Then, "Get those men out of the furnace," he commanded.

"They risked their lives rather than be disloyal to their God.

"I now make this declaration to everyone: there is no god who can rescue like the God of Shadrach, Meshach, and Abednego."

To you alone, O Lord, to you alone,
and not to us, must glory be given
because of your constant love and faithfulness.

Why should the nations ask us,
"Where is your God?"
Our God is in heaven;
he does whatever he wishes.
Their gods are made of silver and gold,
formed by human hands.
They have mouths, but cannot speak,
and eyes, but cannot see.
They have ears, but cannot hear,
and noses, but cannot smell.
They have hands, but cannot feel,
and feet, but cannot walk;
they cannot make a sound.

Trust in the Lord, all you that worship him.
He helps you and protects you.

He will bless everyone who honours him,
the great and the small alike.

PSALM 115:1–8, 11, 13

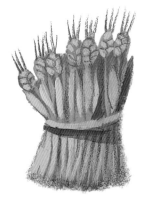

Exile and return

Let those who wept as they sowed their seed
gather the harvest with joy!

PSALM 126:5

WHEN THE PEOPLE of Judah were defeated, they felt desolate. Their great city of Jerusalem and their magnificent Temple were gone. As exiles in Babylon, what could they do to stay faithful to their God?

They turned to their national collection of writings: the Scriptures. Here they could read the stories of days gone by; they could relearn the laws given in ancient times; they could pay attention to the writings of their wise men, the prophets.

They took to meeting on their sabbath day of rest, down by the riverbank. The gathering was called a synagogue, and such meetings became a central part of the Jewish faith.

55

The years went by. The conquerors of the Jews were in turn defeated by the Persians. The all-powerful Persian emperor allowed exiled peoples to return to their own land.

The first band of Jews who returned to the remains of Jerusalem faced many difficulties. Other peoples had made their homes in the region and they resented the new arrivals. They even tried to attack the Jews as they built new city walls.

Nehemiah took charge. He had been a high official in the Persian court. Now he used his wisdom and experience to help his own people. He devised a plan that allowed some people to work on the rebuilding while others stood guard. In this way the city walls were rebuilt. A priest named Ezra led the celebrations by reading aloud from the Law.

"We have forgotten so much!" said the leaders of the
people. "Moses told us always to remember the years when
people lived as wanderers between Egypt and Canaan. Once a year we too
should live as they did."

They made an announcement: "We are going to celebrate the festival of
Shelters. Everyone must go out into the hills to get branches from pines,
olives, myrtles, and palms and use them to build a simple shelter outside their
homes. For seven days everyone will live as a wanderer and remember Moses
and the laws he gave us."

It was a time of joy and hope.

The Jews also built a new Temple in Jerusalem. Like the first, it had an innermost room, but now there was no ark of the covenant to place in it, no tablets of the Law to treasure. Instead, they remembered words from the book of the prophet Isaiah: that the way to treasure God's laws was to obey them.

"WHAT GOD WANTS is for us to obey the Law,"
said the prophet. "If you put an end to
oppression, to every gesture of contempt, and to
every evil word; if you give food to the hungry and
satisfy those who are in need, then the darkness
around you will turn to the brightness of noon. And I
will always guide you and satisfy you with good things.
I will keep you strong and well. You will be like a
garden that has plenty of water, like a spring of water
that never runs dry."

FROM ISAIAH 58:9–11

The child of Bethlehem

The people who walked in darkness have seen a great light.

ISAIAH 9:2

THE JEWISH PEOPLE had been full of hope as they rebuilt their land. Their prophets spoke of future glories, when a king like David would be their salvation: a king who would defeat their enemies and bring them peace and freedom.

Years went by and their hopes dimmed. Once again they were defeated by more powerful nations: first the Greeks, and then the Romans. The land of the Jews was just a small province in a vast empire.

Then, one day, God sent the angel Gabriel to the town of Nazareth, to a young woman named Mary.

"Do not be afraid," said the angel. "God has chosen you to be the mother of his Son: Jesus. He will be a king like his famous ancestor David, and his kingdom will never end."

Mary was astonished: "I can't be a mother!" she said. "I'm not yet married!"

"What I have said can come true because God can make it come true," replied the angel.

"I will do as God wants," said Mary.

Mary was already promised in marriage to a man named Joseph. An angel spoke to him also, asking him to take care of Mary and her baby.

When the order came from the Roman emperor for everyone to take part in a census, Joseph and Mary went as family. They went to Bethlehem, because that was Joseph's home town.

When they arrived, they had to shelter in a stable, because there was no room at the inn. There, Mary's baby was born. She wrapped him in swaddling clothes and laid him in a manger.

There were shepherds out on the hills nearby that night, taking care of their sheep. Suddenly, one of God's angels appeared. "I bring good news," cried the angel. "Tonight, in Bethlehem, a new king has been born. He is the one chosen by God to bring salvation."

For one bright, brilliant moment the sky was filled with angels, singing praises.

Then, when the sky went dark, the shepherds hurried to Bethlehem.

They found the baby just as the angel had said.

From lands far to the east, wise men came riding.

"A new star has appeared," they said to each other. "We believe it will lead us to the child who will one day be king of the Jews.

"We bring rich gifts: gold, frankincense, and myrrh."

The star led them to Bethlehem: to Mary and to Jesus.

A CHILD IS born to us!
A son is given to us!
And he will be our ruler.
He will be called, "Wonderful Counsellor",
"Mighty God", "Eternal Father", "Prince of Peace".
His royal power will continue to grow;
his kingdom will always be at peace.
He will rule as King David's successor,
basing his power on right and justice,
from now until the end of time.

ISAIAH 9:6–7

The kingdom of God

Jesus said, "Be concerned above everything else with the kingdom of God and with what God requires of you."

MATTHEW 6:33

JESUS GREW UP with Mary and Joseph in Nazareth. He learned to be a carpenter, but he always knew that God had other work for him to do. One day, Jesus was in the synagogue in Nazareth. It was his turn to read aloud from the Scriptures. He read from the book of the prophet Isaiah.

"The spirit of the Lord is upon me,
because he has chosen me to bring good news to the poor.
He has sent me to proclaim liberty to the captives
and recovery of sight to the blind;
to set free the oppressed
and announce that the time has come
when the Lord will save his people."

Jesus looked at the people with whom he had grown up. "Today," he said, "those words have come true."

The townsfolk could not believe that Jesus was God's chosen one. Before they could harm him, Jesus slipped away.

He went to Capernaum, on the shore of Lake Galilee. He chose four fishermen – Peter and Andrew, James and John – to join him as disciples to help him gather people in God's kingdom.

Crowds gathered to listen to Jesus. "I haven't come to do away with the Law of Moses and the teachings of the prophets," he said, "but to make them come true.

"Don't take revenge on those who wrong you. If a Roman soldier makes you carry his pack for one mile, offer to carry it for two.

"You know it's right to love your friends. Now I am telling you to love your enemies as well.

"If you choose to do good and charitable deeds, do them in such a way that no one except God notices.

"Do not judge others. God alone has the right to judge a person by what they do.

"Do not worry about money and the things it can buy.

"Look at the flowers: God clothes them in petals lovelier than any royal robes.

"Look at the birds: God provides the food they need.

"If God takes care of the birds and flowers, you can be sure that God will take care of you.

"Don't show off about how religious you are. When you pray, go to your room and close the door.

"Don't say long and complicated prayers. God already knows what you need. Instead, say these words:

> Our Father in heaven,
> hallowed be your name,
> your kingdom come,
> your will be done,
> on earth as in heaven.
> Give us today our daily bread.
> Forgive us our sins
> as we forgive those who sin against us.
> Lead us not into temptation
> but deliver us from evil.

"Remember this," said Jesus. "If you forgive others the wrong they have done to you, then God will forgive your wrongdoing. If you don't forgive others, then God will not forgive you."

All kinds of people came to listen to Jesus' teaching – from the most important in society to the least.

One day some mothers came to Jesus.

"What are you here for?" the disciples asked.

"We'd like Jesus to give our children a blessing," they answered.

"Jesus is far too busy to do such a thing!" exclaimed the disciples.

Jesus heard the conversation.

"Let the children come to me, and do not try to stop them," he said. "The kingdom of God belongs to such as these."

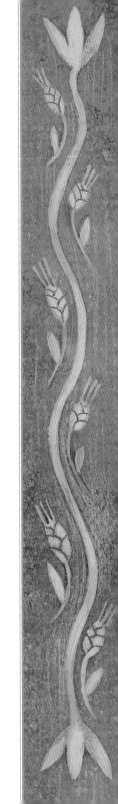

T HE DISCIPLES CAME to Jesus, asking, "Who is the greatest in the kingdom of heaven?"

So Jesus called a child, made him stand in front of them, and said, "I assure you that unless you change and become like children, you will never enter the kingdom of heaven. The greatest in the kingdom of heaven is the one who humbles himself and becomes like this child. And whoever welcomes in my name one such child as this, welcomes me."

MATTHEW 18:1–5

The good Samaritan

Jesus said, "Do for others just what you want them to do for you."

LUKE 6:31

JESUS OFTEN SPOKE about God's love and forgiveness. People who knew their lives were not perfect were enthusiastic. Not so enthusiastic were the people who were very religious, who were strict about obeying God's laws.

One day, a teacher of the Law came to Jesus with a question. He was hoping that Jesus would answer it badly and show that he wasn't an expert.

"What must I do to have eternal life?" he asked.

"What do the Scriptures say?" Jesus asked him.

"That's simple," said the man. "We must love God with all our being, and we must love our neighbour as ourselves."

"Quite right," said Jesus. "That's all you have to do."

The man was annoyed that his question had been dealt with so quickly.

"But who is my neighbour?" he protested.

Jesus told a story.

"There was once a man who was going from Jerusalem to Jericho. On the way, robbers ambushed him. They robbed him and left him for dead in the road.

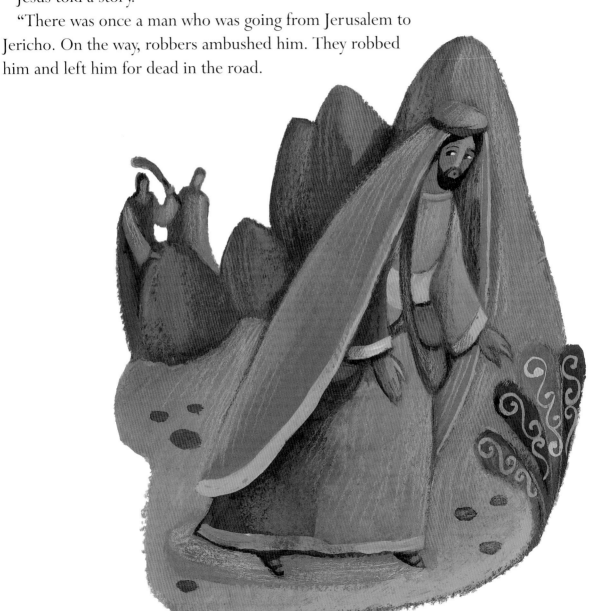

"A priest from the Temple came along. He saw the man, but hurried on by.

"A helper from the Temple came next. He came closer to look at the man. Then he too hurried away.

"A Samaritan came by."

(Everyone knew that Samaritans were not Jews at all. They never went to the Temple to worship…

so what would they know about keeping God's laws?)

"He saw the man and felt sorry for him. He went over to the man and bandaged his wounds. Then he lifted him onto his donkey and brought him to an inn, where he took care of him.

"The following day, the Samaritan had to travel on. Before he left, he gave the innkeeper some money. 'This is to pay you to look after the man,' he said. 'If you need to spend more, I will give you the extra next time I come.'

"Now," said Jesus. "In your opinion, which of the three passers-by was a neighbour to the man in need?"

"The one who was kind to him," came the answer.

"Then you go and do the same," said Jesus.

Dᴇᴀʀ Gᴏᴅ,
When I see someone in need,
may I know when to stop and help
and when to hurry to fetch help;
but may I never pass by,
pretending I did not see.

ʙᴀꜱᴇᴅ ᴏɴ ᴛʜᴇ ᴘᴀʀᴀʙʟᴇ ᴏꜰ ᴛʜᴇ ɢᴏᴏᴅ ꜱᴀᴍᴀʀɪᴛᴀɴ, ʟᴜᴋᴇ 10:25–37

Tʜᴇ ᴡɪꜱᴅᴏᴍ ꜰʀᴏᴍ above is pure first of all; it is also
peaceful, gentle, and friendly; it is full of compassion
and produces a harvest of good deeds; it is free from
prejudice and hypocrisy. And goodness is the harvest that is
produced from the seeds the peacemakers plant in peace.

ᴊᴀᴍᴇꜱ 3:17–18

Rich man, poor man

Jesus said, "You cannot serve both God and money."

LUKE 16:13

J ESUS TOLD THIS story to warn people not to put their trust in money:
"There was once a very rich man. He had a fine house, fine clothes, fine food… and the very best of everything.

"It so happened that in the same town there lived a beggar named Lazarus. He was suffering from a horrible skin disease that left him covered with open sores, and totally unable to make a living.

"Every day Lazarus asked to be carried to a place outside the rich man's house. Every day he hoped that someone in the household would leave some of the kitchen scraps for him to eat. The town's stray dogs came to the same place. Sometimes they would lick the sores on Lazarus' body.

"In time the poor man died. Angels came and carried him to heaven. There he was treated with the greatest respect, and given a place at the heavenly feast right next to the father of his nation – Abraham, of days gone by.

"The rich man also died. No angels came to carry him to heaven. Instead, he was taken down to the fire of Hades, the world of the dead.

"He looked up and saw the poor man enjoying all the delights of heaven.

"'Father Abraham,' he called, 'take pity on me. Please send Lazarus to bring me a few drops of water to cool my parched mouth. I am in such pain down here.'

"Abraham looked at the rich man sternly. 'Remember,' he said, 'how you used to enjoy the good things in life while Lazarus suffered? Now things are the other way around. What is more, there is a pit between you and us that no one can cross.'

"The rich man sighed the deepest sigh. Then he spoke again. 'Then let me ask this of you, father Abraham. Send Lazarus to my father's house. Tell him to warn my five brothers so they can do what is required to be welcome in heaven, and not this place of torment.'

"Abraham shook his head: 'Your brothers only have to obey the teachings of Moses and the prophets,' he said.

"'Those teachings are not enough,' complained the rich man, "but if someone were to come back from the dead and warn them, they would turn away from wrongdoing.'

"'Not so,' replied Abraham. 'A person who will not pay attention to the teachings of Moses and the prophets will not be convinced even if someone were to rise from the dead.'"

J ESUS SAID THIS:

"Do not store up riches for yourselves here on earth, where moths and rust destroy, and robbers break in and steal. Instead, store up riches for yourselves in heaven, where moths and rust cannot destroy, and robbers cannot break in and steal. For your heart will always be where your riches are."

MATTHEW 6:19–21

Servants of the king

Jesus said, "Many who now are first will be last, and many who now are last will be first."

MATTHEW 19:30

ONE DAY A wealthy young man came to Jesus.

"Teacher," he said. "What must I do to have eternal life?"

"You must keep the great commandments that God has given our people," replied Jesus.

"Oh, I already do that!" said the young man. "What else is required?"

Jesus looked at the man with a steady gaze. "You must sell all your possessions and then come and follow me," he said.

The man's face fell. "I'll… I'll need to think more about that," he said. And with that he walked away.

Jesus sighed to disciples. "It is hard for those who are wealthy to let go of their comfortable lives to come and be part of God's kingdom. It is only because of God's mercy and grace that anyone can do so.

"Yet God will greatly reward those who do.

"There was once a man who owned a vineyard. When it was time to harvest the grapes, he needed to hire extra workers. First thing in the morning he went down to the marketplace where those who wanted a job were waiting hopefully.

" 'Come with me,' he said to them. 'I will pay a good wage: a silver coin for a day's work.'

"The men were delighted. They went to the vineyard and worked diligently.

"The owner of the vineyard watched thoughtfully. 'I'm going to need even more help,' he said. 'I'll go and hire some more workers.'

"He went back to the marketplace at nine o'clock and found more people eager for hire.

"He went again at noon, then at three, and as late as five o'clock in the afternoon.

"Those who came all did exactly as they were asked.

"As the sun began to sink down, the foreman came with bags of money to pay the workers. 'I will call you in reverse order of when you were hired,' he declared.

"First to collect their pay were those who had been hired at five o'clock. Each received a silver coin.

"The men from the early morning whispered excitedly. 'It looks like the rate of pay has gone up,' they said. 'I wonder what we'll get?'

"When their turn came, they each received a silver coin.

" 'That can't be right,' they grumbled. 'We've slaved through the heat of the day, and we get the same as the ones who arrived last.'

"The owner of the vineyard stepped forward. 'Why are you complaining?' he asked sharply. 'You have been given the wage we agreed. No more, no less.

" 'I have the right to do as I wish with my money.

" 'What right have you to be jealous if I am generous?' "

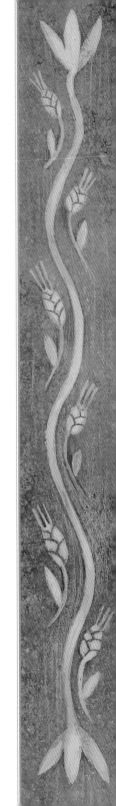

O N ANOTHER OCCASION, Jesus told his followers more about what it meant to be servants in God's kingdom with these words.

"Suppose one of you has a servant who is ploughing or looking after the sheep. When he comes in from the field, do you tell him to hurry and eat his meal? Of course not! Instead, you say to him, 'Get my supper ready, then put on your apron and wait on me while I eat and drink; after that you may have your meal.'

"The servant does not deserve thanks for obeying orders, does he?

"It is the same with you; when you have done all you have been told to do, say, 'We are ordinary servants; we have only done our duty.'"

LUKE 17:7–10

The Last Supper

Jesus said, "And now I give you a new commandment: love one another."

JOHN 13:34

FOR THREE YEARS Jesus preached his message. Wherever he went with his chosen band of twelve disciples, crowds gathered. Some were eager to hear his teaching; others were eager to find fault with it. Some came to be healed; others simply wanted to see if Jesus really could heal the sick with just a touch.

So, when Jesus and his disciples came to Jerusalem for the Passover, it was no surprise that crowds noticed.

It started with a whisper. "Look! Jesus is riding a donkey. In the book of the prophet Zechariah it says that God's chosen king will ride a donkey when he comes to claim Jerusalem."

As the whisper spread, the crowd grew excited. They cut palm branches and waved them. "God bless the king!" they cried.

The people who mistrusted Jesus – teachers and other leaders of the people – frowned deeply.

93

When Jesus reached Jerusalem, he went to the Temple. The festival market, hoping to make money from those who had come to the Temple to celebrate the Passover, was in full swing.

Jesus overturned the tables of the sellers and drove them out.

"The Temple is meant to be a house of prayer!" he said. "You have made it a den of thieves!"

Once again, the leaders of the people were furious. But what could they do? Jesus was always surrounded by adoring crowds.

Jesus knew what his enemies were thinking, and that they were determined to get rid of him.

He asked his disciples to prepare a festival meal.

As they gathered in an upstairs room, Jesus tied a towel around his waist and did the job of a servant: he washed his disciples' dusty feet.

When he had finished, he explained. "You call me Teacher and Lord, but I have acted as your servant.

"Remember my example, and serve one another in humble ways."

The meal itself was a time to remember the time of Moses: the people's escape from Egypt, the giving of the Law, and the covenant.

Jesus took a piece of bread, gave thanks to God, broke it, and said to his disciples, "This is my body, which is for you. Do this in memory of me."

In the same way after supper he took the cup of wine and said, "This cup is God's new covenant, sealed with my blood. Whenever you drink it, do so in memory of me."

As he said these words, Jesus was foretelling his own death, but the disciples did not want to hear that message. All except one of them wanted to believe that their master was God's chosen king.

J ESUS' BODY,
Broken bread,
By God's word
We all are fed.

Jesus' lifeblood,
Wine that's spilt,
As one temple
We are built.

At this table
Take your place:
Feast upon
God's love and grace.

The story of the cross

Jesus said, "I am the way, the truth, and the life."

JOHN 14:6

AFTER THE SUPPER, Jesus and his faithful disciples went out to sleep under the stars, in an olive grove named Gethsemane.

But one disciple had agreed to betray Jesus to his enemies: Judas Iscariot slipped away from the group. When he came to the garden, he brought armed men to arrest his master.

The Temple priests and leaders of the people put Jesus on trial. "Is it true that you tell people you are God's promised king?" they demanded to know. "Are you saying you are the messiah, the Christ?"

Jesus would not answer them. He already knew what was going to happen: they wanted him put to death, and for that they needed the agreement of the Roman governor in Jerusalem, Pontius Pilate.

Pilate himself questioned Jesus: "Are you the king of the Jews, as your enemies say?" he asked.

"My kingdom does not belong to this world," replied Jesus. "If it did, my followers would fight for me. But that is not the case."

Pilate gave his verdict to the Jewish leaders. "I see no reason to condemn this man," he said. "I have the authority to release a prisoner for Passover. Shall I set him free?"

But by now a crowd had gathered: an angry crowd who believed what Jesus' accusers had told them.

"Crucify him," they cried.

Pilate gave the order. His soldiers took Jesus away.

Jesus was forced to carry his cross to the place of execution: Golgotha. There, his hands and feet were nailed to the rough wood. Jesus was hung up to die, along with two criminals.

Even as he struggled to breathe, Jesus said a prayer for his enemies: "Father, forgive them. They don't know what they are doing."

Just before the sun went down, friends came and took Jesus' body. They laid it in a tomb and rolled the stone door shut.

Then they hurried away: the weekly day of rest, the sabbath, was about to begin.

101

Very early on Sunday morning, some women went back to the tomb. They wanted to wrap the body of Jesus in the proper manner for its long decay.

When they reached the place, the stone door of the tomb was open. Inside were angels.

"Why have you come to this place of death to look for someone who is alive?" the angels asked. "Jesus is not here: he is risen."

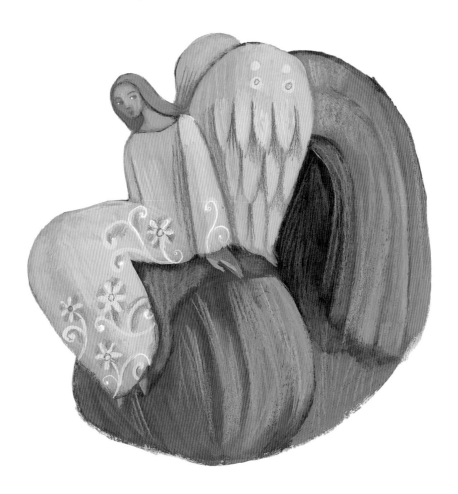

JESUS SAID:

"Do not be worried and upset. Believe in God and believe also in me. There are many rooms in my Father's house, and I am going to prepare a place for you. I would not tell you this if it were not so. And after I go and prepare a place for you, I will come back and take you to myself, so that you will be where I am. You know the way that leads to the place where I am going."

JOHN 14:1–4

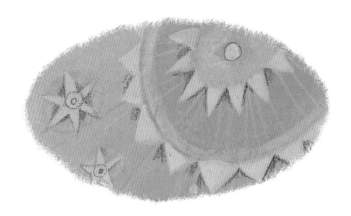

The Holy Spirit

Jesus said, "If you love me, you will obey my commandments.
I will ask the Father, and he will give you another Helper, who will stay with
you for ever. He is the Spirit who reveals the truth about God."

JOHN 14:15–17

AFTER JESUS WAS raised from the dead, he appeared many times to his disciples. "It is for you to spread the message about God's kingdom now," he told them. "But wait for the right time. God's Holy Spirit will come upon you and give you the wisdom and courage you need."

One day, as they were gathered on a hillside, a cloud came and wrapped itself around Jesus.

The disciples were looking up in wonder when two angels appeared.

"Why are you looking at the sky?" they asked. "Jesus has been taken into heaven. One day, he will return in the same way that you have seen him go."

For the next ten days, Jesus' followers felt lost. Jesus had gone. The people who had had him put to death were probably hunting them down. They felt too afraid to go out and about, let alone preach about God's kingdom.

One day, all the believers were together in a locked room. They heard a sound like a strong wind, and saw flames of fire dancing above their heads.

They were all filled with God's Holy Spirit. By a miracle, they were able to speak in other languages, and they felt ready to take the message of God's kingdom out into the world.

The disciple named Peter addressed the people of Jerusalem that very day.

"Each one of you must turn away from your sins and be baptized in the name of Jesus Christ, so that your sins will be forgiven; and you will receive God's gift, the Holy Spirit."

Thousands of people believed his words.

S PIRIT OF GOD, put love in my life.
Spirit of God, put joy in my life.
Spirit of God, put peace in my life.

Spirit of God, make me patient.
Spirit of God, make me kind.
Spirit of God, make me good.

Spirit of God, give me faithfulness.
Spirit of God, give me humility.
Spirit of God, give me self-control.

BASED ON GALATIANS 5:22–23

New believers

Jesus said, "Go to all peoples everywhere and make them my disciples; baptize them in the name of the Father, the Son, and the Holy Spirit, and teach them to obey everything I have commanded you."

MATTHEW 28:19–20

JESUS' FAITHFUL DISCIPLES were greatly strengthened by God's Holy Spirit. They began to spread the good news about God's kingdom far and wide. Those who had rejected Jesus were alarmed to see how many people believed it. Among them was a Jewish scholar named Saul. He was on his way to Damascus, to have the believers there arrested, when a sudden light blinded him. He heard Jesus speaking: "Why are you being so cruel to me?"

When Saul reached Damascus, one of the believers came to heal him. Saul became an enthusiastic believer. Using the Roman version of his name, Paul, he began preaching about Jesus.

He made long journeys to many parts of the Roman empire. His travels took him to Philippi in Macedonia. There, by the river, he came across some Jews who had gathered to pray. Among them was a wealthy businesswoman named Lydia. When she heard what Paul had to say about Jesus, she asked to be baptized as a believer.

She welcomed Paul and his companions to her house and took care of them. The place soon became a meeting place for other believers: a church.

Because they believed that Jesus was God's chosen king – the messiah, the Christ – believers all over the empire became known as Christians.

Those who were wise in the new faith wanted to teach and encourage others. Paul wrote letters to the churches he had started. Here are some that he wrote to the church in Philippi:

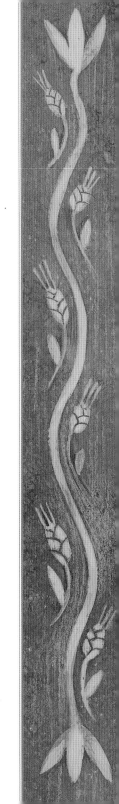

MAY YOU ALWAYS be joyful in your union with the Lord. I say it again: rejoice!

Show a gentle attitude towards everyone. The Lord is coming soon. Don't worry about anything, but in all your prayers ask God for what you need, always asking him with a thankful heart. And God's peace, which is far beyond human understanding, will keep your hearts and minds safe in union with Christ Jesus.

Fill your mind with those things that are good and that deserve praise; things that are true, noble, right, pure, lovely, and honourable. Put into practice what you learned and received from me, both from my words and from my actions.

And the God who gives us peace will be with you.

PAUL'S LETTER TO THE PHILIPPIANS 4:4–7, 8–9

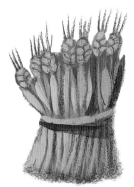

Belonging to the church

Paul wrote: "There is no difference between Jews and Gentiles, between slaves and free people, between men and women; you are all one in union with Christ Jesus.

"You are the descendants of Abraham and will receive what God has promised."

GALATIANS 3:28–29

PAUL ESTABLISHED CHURCHES throughout the Roman empire, but he also made enemies. They had him arrested. Paul asked to be taken to Rome, to be put on trial in the emperor's court.

While he waited, he became part of the church in Rome. His preaching made several converts. Among them was a young man named Onesimus. He had been a slave in Colossae but had run away.

When Paul pieced together his story, he knew he had to act.

"You've been a great help to me here," Paul told him, "and I think of you as a son. But you still belong to your master, and here's the thing: I know him. He's a Christian now.

"I'm going to send you back, and I'm going to ask him to welcome you."

Onesimus went, carrying Paul's letter. He still felt nervous as he stood in front of his old master Philemon, watching his face as he read what Paul had written.

Philemon finished reading and looked up.

"Welcome back," he said simply. "The faith we now share has changed everything. You're not just a slave; you are also my dear brother in Christ.

"I've learned a few things myself while you were away. I've learned that God is my master in heaven. As a master of a household here, I need to be fair and just."

Onesimus breathed a sigh of relief, but there was something he had to confess.

"I did help myself to a bit of cash when I ran away," he said. "Paul said I had to tell you. He said he'd pay what I owe."

Philemon smiled. "He put the offer in his letter," he said. "But I owe my faith to Paul. I'm not going to ask for any money."

Everything worked out as it should. Those of Philemon's friends who were not Christians had once laughed at his faith.

"Whatever we thought of the teachings, they've certainly changed the old man for the better," they agreed. "It makes you think."

P AUL WROTE THIS to the church in Colossae:
"You are the people of God; he loved you and chose
you for his own. So then, you must clothe yourselves with
compassion, kindness, humility, gentleness, and patience.
Be tolerant with one another and forgive one another
whenever any of you has a complaint against someone else.

"You must forgive one another just as the Lord has
forgiven you. And to all these qualities add love, which
binds all things together in perfect unity."

COLOSSIANS 3:12–14

The new Jerusalem

Jesus said, "Happy are those who are persecuted because they do what God requires; the kingdom of heaven belongs to them!"

MATTHEW 5:10

CHURCH MEETINGS COULD go on for a long time. The children found it hard to pay attention. Today the grown-ups were reading a long, long letter from someone named John.

It had begun simply enough: telling Christians from different churches not to be discouraged.

"Even though people are mean to us because we're Christians," whispered the eldest child, "we mustn't be mean back. We've got to be kind and forgiving, whatever happens."

"But it's hard," replied a younger child. "Sometimes it's like everything that's wicked is winning."

As the children listened, it seemed that John must have thought the same. But John was describing a great battle between good and evil: a battle in which the great angel Michael led the other angels to fight a dragon — the Devil, Satan — and threw him and his followers out of heaven to earth.

"But that means that wickedness is here on earth," a little girl began to cry.

"Well, for now," said the eldest child. "But listen. I'm sure it will be beaten in the end."

125

They listened in awe as they heard these words from John.

"I saw a new heaven and new earth. And I saw the Holy City, the new Jerusalem, coming down out of heaven from God.

"And I heard a voice: 'Now God's home is with human beings! He will be with them, and they shall be his people. God himself will be with them, and he will be their God. He will wipe away all tears from their eyes. There will be no more death, no more grief or crying or pain.

" 'Listen,' says Jesus, 'I am coming soon! I will bring my rewards with me, to give each one according to what he has done. I am the first and the last, the beginning and the end.' "

REVELATION 21:1–2, 3–4; 22:12

MAY THE GRACE of the Lord Jesus be with everyone.

REVELATION 22:21